a book for
Elie

a book for Elie

Rhoda Trooboff • Pictures by Anna Nazaretz Radjou

Tenley Circle Press • Washington, DC

Cataloging in Publication Data
Trooboff, Rhoda.
A book for Elie.

ISBN 978 0 9773536 1 3

Library of Congress Control Number: 2008909341

Tenley Circle Press, Ltd.
P.O. Box 5625, Friendship Station, Washington, D.C. 20016
www.tenleycirclepress.com

For the *real* Elie

Just before naptime on a late winter Wednesday,
Elie and Grandpa were having a jolly time reading about lizards.
Grandpa said the words. Elie looked at the pictures.
They took turns turning the pages.
Elie's toy lizard Woody cuddled with them.

Grandpa showed Elie a picture of a lizard without a tail.
"Poor little lizard," Grandpa said.
"But lizards can lose a tail and grow another.
Good things take time."

Grandpa carried Elie to his crib.

"Time for a nap, little one," Grandpa said.

"We'll play again later. Play is even nicer after a sweet snooze."

Elie snuggled with Woody and fell asleep.

Zzzzzzz

In the living room, Grandma was sitting with a notebook in her lap.
Her face crinkled into a frown.
She was chewing the end of her pencil.
"What shall I write now?" she fussed. "All my ideas have dried up."

"Good ideas take time," Grandpa said. "They'll come after a good rest."

Grandma and Grandpa settled in for a nap. Grandma snoozed on the sofa.
Grandpa rested in the recliner chair.

Elie woke up and let out a hoot. He flipped Woody from his crib. Woody landed with a thud.

Grandpa woke up.

Grandma had an idea. "Aha!" she said.

thud.

crumple...

crumple...

crumple...

The next Wednesday Grandpa and Elie played while Grandma wrote.
She smiled as she worked. She wrote and erased and wrote some more.

Grandma tossed crumpled papers into the wastebasket.
Some papers tumbled onto the floor near Woody.
Grandpa and Elie made them part of their game.

The next Wednesday Elie and Grandpa went to the library.
They returned old books and got new ones.
While they were gone, Grandma worked on her new book.

Grandpa and Elie came home from the library.
They read while Grandma made lunch. Grandpa said the words.
Elie pointed at the pictures. They took turns turning the pages.
Woody seemed to listen.

After lunch everyone yawned. "We all need naps," Grandpa said.

Elie rubbed his eyes and shook his head. "No nap," he said.

"We'll play again later," Grandpa said.
"Everything's better after a nice rest."

Another week passed.

Late on Wednesday night Grandma's artist friend Anna sat at her computer reading her email.

Here is what she read:

Dear Anna,

Take out your ink and pens and paints and brushes!

Get a good night's sleep! I'll send you the story in the morning!

It's about a lizard named Woody, who loses his tail and grows another!

　　Love,

　　Rhoda

Anna googled LIZARD. She giggled at what she saw.

She made a few sketches and yawned.

"Ideas are better after a good night's sleep," she said.

She fell asleep and dreamed of lizards.

Wednesdays passed one after another.

Winter turned to spring. Summer slipped by, and fall followed.

Elie grew from a baby into a little boy.

He still had a jolly time reading books with Grandpa before lunch.

Now Elie said all the words.

Woody looked a little the worse for wear.

Elie still took naps with Woody, but now they slept in a
big-boy bed.

vroom
vroooom

On a winter Wednesday, just after their weekly walk to the library, Elie and Grandpa played doctor with Woody.

Suddenly the phone made a loud sound. Grandma took the call.

Grandma put down the phone.

"Lunch is on the table!" she shouted.

"I'm off to the print shop! Anna emailed the book files this morning! I can't wait!"

"Shouldn't you have lunch?" Grandpa asked.

"I can't wait!" Grandma repeated. "It's too exciting!"

She jumped into her little roadster and took off up the street.

bzzzzzzzzzz

bzzzzzzzzzzz

bzzzzzzzzzzz

rrumble

Grandma entered the print shop. The press buzzed loudly.

Ben turned from the control panel to Grandma. "I got your files from Anna!" He shouted over the noise.

"I'll run a sample right away!"

"You're very busy right now," Grandma said.

She looked at the clock.

It was past lunchtime. Her tummy rumbled.

"Shouldn't you slow down and stop for lunch?" she asked.

"You're right," Ben said. "Work goes better after a break." He pressed a button on the press.

The machine went silent.

Suddenly the shop was very peaceful.

Grandma smiled.

"I'll come back after lunch and my nap," she said.

It was a late-winter Wednesday morning.

Elie and Woody were on safari in a sunny corner.

Grandpa was reading the newspaper.

The phone interrupted the quiet.

"Hello?" Grandma said. "Yes?" Her face lit up in a smile.

Grandpa looked up from the newspaper.

Elie peeked out from his tent.

"Today?" Grandma's voice was excited.

"Yes, we'll be home all afternoon.

Send one box here, please,
and ship the rest to the warehouse.

I'll tell them to expect nineteen boxes.

Thank you."

She hung up the phone.

"Are you two ready for lunch?" she asked.

"Elie, would you like to take
your nap in your tent?"

"Yes," said Elie.

"Can Grandpa come, too?"

100
COPIES

After naptime Elie opened his eyes. He peeked out of his tent.
A box sat by the door. It had a label.

Nineteen boxes rode inside a truck.
Each box had a label.

At the warehouse nineteen boxes rode on a forklift onto a high shelf.
Each box had a label.

Wednesdays passed. Winter turned to spring.

In the warehouse ten copies of *A Tail for Woody* scooted along a roller belt into a box.

The box rode in a truck to the town where Elie lived.

One Wednesday morning in spring,
Elie and Grandpa went into the bookshop.
When they came out, Elie was carrying a bag.
They crossed the street and went into the library.

Elie gave the librarian a book from his bag.
"This is for your library," Elie said.

"Thank you," said the librarian.
"Would you like to be the first person to borrow it?" he asked.

"Yes, please," said Elie.

a tail for woody

The librarian stamped the book and handed it to Elie.

"Thank you," said Elie.

"You're welcome," the librarian said. "See you next Wednesday."

Grandpa and Elie went home. Grandma had lunch on the table.

After lunch Elie and Grandpa had a jolly time reading.
Elie said the words. Grandpa pointed at the pictures.
They took turns turning the pages. Woody listened.

Grandma sat on the sofa. She was chewing the end of her pencil.
"What shall I write?" she asked. "What'll my next story be?"

Grandpa and Elie smiled.

"Sleep on it, Grandma," Elie said. "Good things take time."

Grandpa, Grandma, and Elie settled down for a good rest.

They dreamt of tales that might come next.

So did Woody.

TEXT BY
Rhoda Trooboff

ILLUSTRATIONS & DESIGN BY
Anna Nazaretz Radjou

PRINTING & BINDING BY
Beacon Printing Company, Inc., Waldorf, MD, USA

RECYCLED WOOD PROVIDED BY
Case Design/Remodeling, Inc.,
the artist, and her father

LUCIDA SANS FONT (BODY TYPE)
designed by Kris Holmes & Charles Bigelow

MINYA NOUVELLE FONT (DISPLAY TYPE)
designed by Ray Larabie

Beacon Printing Company, Inc. (Waldorf, MD, USA) enforces a strict recycling program and is committed to worker safety and health as an integral part of its business plan. Beacon is FSC (Forest Stewardship Council) certified and uses paper from responsibly managed forests and other controlled sources. The inks used in printing this book are vegetable based, not made from petroleum products.

Mixed Sources
Product group from well-managed
forests, controlled sources and
recycled wood or fibre
www.fsc.org Cert no. SGS-COC-004246
© 1996 Forest Stewardship Council

Rhoda Trooboff is a long-time teacher, author, poet, wife, mother, and grandmother who lives in Washington, DC. Her first picture book is *Ben, the Bells and the Peacocks.*

Anna Nazaretz Radjou is an illustrator, graphic designer, and artist living and working in Northern Virginia. She graduated with a BFA in Illustration from the Maryland Institute College of Art.

Rhoda and Anna thank their families and friends for their support throughout the process of making this book.

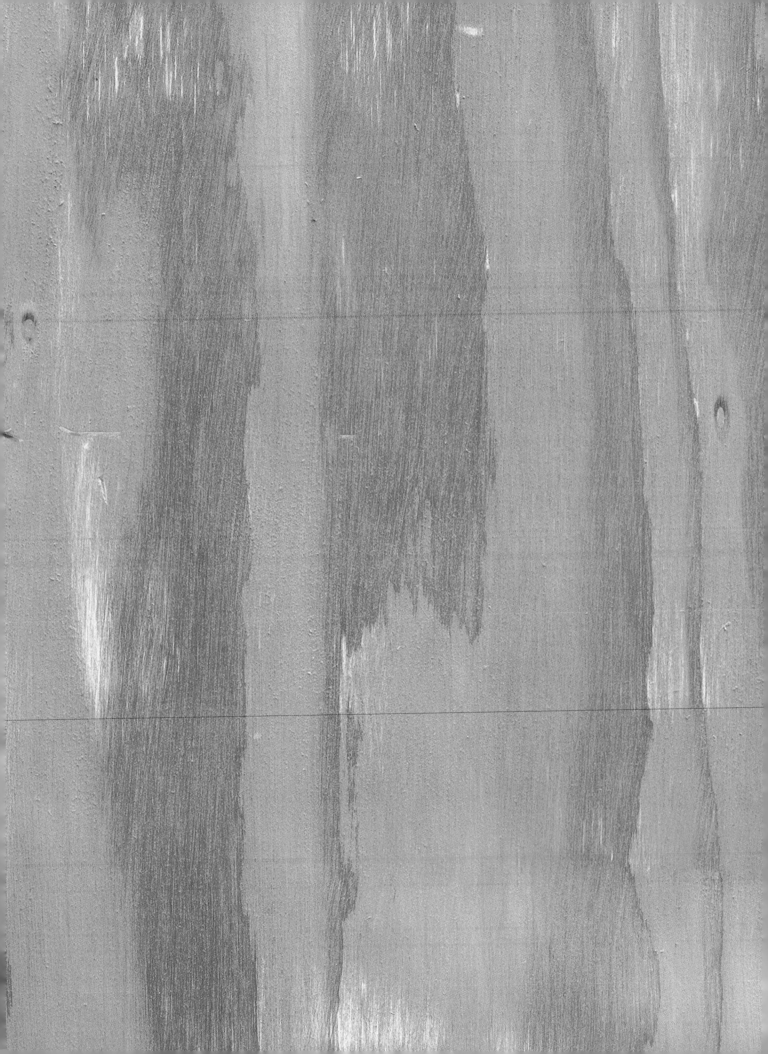